AT THE
HEELS OF HISTORY

Bo-Bo's Cave of Gold

Also by Pam Berkman and Dorothy Hearst

Filigree's Midnight Ride

WITHDRAWN

AT THE
HEELS OF HISTORY

Bo-Bo's Cave of Gold

Pam Berkman and Dorothy Hearst

Illustrated by Claire Powell

Margaret K. McElderry Books

New York London Toronto Sydney New Delhi

MARGARET K. McELDERRY BOOKS

An imprint of Simon & Schuster Children's Publishing Division

1230 Avenue of the Americas, New York, New York 10020

MARGARET K. McELDERRY BOOKS is a trademark of Simon & Schuster, Inc.

For information about special discounts for bulk purchases, please contact Simon & Schuster Special Sales at 1-866-506-1949 or business@simonandschuster.com.

The Simon & Schuster Speakers Bureau can bring authors to your live event. For more information or to book an event, contact the Simon & Schuster Speakers Bureau at 1-866-248-3049 or visit our website at www.simonspeakers.com.

Also available in a Margaret K. McElderry Books paperback edition

Book design by Debra Sfetsios-Conover and Rebecca Syracuse

The text for this book was set in Caslon Old Face BT.

Cover art has been rendered by hand and colored in Photoshop. All interior illustrations have been drawn by hand using pencil and graphite.

Manufactured in the United States of America

0320 FFG

First Margaret K. McElderry Books hardcover edition April 2020

2 4 6 8 10 9 7 5 3 1

Library of Congress Cataloging-in-Publication Data

Names: Berkman, Pamela, author. | Hearst, Dorothy, 1966– author. | Powell, Claire, illustrator.

Title: Bo-Bo's cave of gold / Pam Berkman and Dorothy Hearst ; illustrated by Claire Powell.

Description: First edition. | New York : Margaret K. McElderry Books, [2020] | Series: At the heels of history | Audience: Ages 6–9. | Audience: Grades 2–3. | Summary: In 1852 California, stray mutt Bo-Bo and his friend, ten-year-old gold prospector Sheng, must risk great danger seeking a rumored treasure after Bo-Bo's kindness leads Sheng into debt.

Identifiers: LCCN 2019031567 (print) | ISBN 9781534433359 (pbk) | ISBN 9781534433366 (hardcover) | ISBN 9781534433373 (eBook)

Subjects: CYAC: Dogs—Fiction. | Gold mines and mining—Fiction. | Chinese Americans—Fiction. | Swindlers and swindling—Fiction. | California—History—1846–1850—Fiction.

Classification: LCC PZ7.1.B457 Bo 2020 (print) | DDC [Fic]—dc23 LC record available at https://lccn.loc.gov/2019031567

To my sisters and brothers—Brenna and

Jimmy, Felice and Howard

–P. B.

To my family, friends, and to all of the dogs.

–D. H.

1
The Pack

1852, Sierra Nevada foothills, California

Sage stood alone under the big oak tree. She looked at her pack one more time.

Maybe they would call her back. Maybe they were just making sure she had learned her lesson. Maybe they didn't really mean she had been thrown out of the pack.

For good.

"I'm sorry," she woofed again.

Her tail usually curled proudly over her back. Now it drooped. Her scruffy ears fell flat against her head.

Acorn, her best friend, looked at the ground. He had the same short fur as Sage,

but a darker golden brown. Racer, a tall terrier, turned away. Cougar, Juniper, and the rest of the dogs watched her across the stretch of grass and manzanita bushes.

Thunder, the pack leader, lifted her lip.

"Get out of here and don't come back!" the big hound growled. Snarling, she held up her left front paw. Her leg had been hurt that morning. Because of Sage.

"You're weak," Thunder barked. "Soft. We have no place for a dog who puts some scraggly two-legged creature ahead of her own pack."

That morning, they had raided a miner's camp for food. Sage had found a large wooden box that smelled like meat. She'd unlatched it with her nose and lifted up the lid with her front paws. She'd pulled out a packet of dried venison. A very old, very thin man rushed over to her. He looked so panicked to see his food being taken away, Sage couldn't do it. She'd dropped the venison.

Thunder had run up to her at just that moment.

"Get that meat!" she'd barked.

Sage had hesitated. That gave the man time to grab his rifle. He fired. The two dogs ran as fast as they could. But the shot grazed Thunder's leg. She was going to be limping for a long time.

Acorn spoke up. "Sage just thought it wasn't right to—"

"Quiet!" Thunder snapped. "Or you can leave too."

Cougar and Juniper growled. Acorn lowered his ears.

Maybe Thunder was right. Maybe Sage shouldn't have cared that the man was hungry. She started to explain one more time.

"I'll be tough on other creatures from now on," she woofed.

She might as well have been talking to a boulder.

"Stay out of our territory," Thunder

warned. "If you ever come near Scrub Hill again, you'll be sorry."

Thunder barked twice. The pack trotted away. None of them looked back. Not even Acorn.

Sage picked her way down the grassy hill. When she got to the riverbank, she passed the old tree stump with the twigs sticking out of it. The twigs looked like long ears and a short tail. Jackrabbit Stump. It marked the end of her pack's territory and all she had ever known.

She walked on. There was nothing else she could do.

2
Sheng

Sage lifted her head and then set it down again. She was curled up in a little hollow on a hillside. She was hungry, but she didn't feel like looking for food.

Since she'd been sent away from the pack, the moon had shrunk from a full circle to a sliver, then grown full again. She'd wandered the hills alone. She'd eaten whatever scraps she could find.

Now she didn't even feel like doing that.

"Nobody cares if I'm alive," she woofed aloud.

"Mopey, miserable mutt," someone said from behind her. She heard a squawk and a whistle. Then something pulled her tail. She yelped and turned to look. No one was there.

She stood and turned the other way. She didn't see anything there, either.

"Hey!" Sage barked.

The something poked her on her shoulder. Then it nipped her tail. It jabbed her back left paw. Sage chased her tail around and around until she didn't know which end of her was the back and which was the front.

She ran out of the hollow.

A bird landed in front of her. It was smaller than a hawk or vulture, more like the size of a dove. But it had a sleek, dome-shaped head and a short, hooked beak. It was drenched in as many colors as Sage knew there were in the world.

She sniffed it. It bit her nose.

"Stop that!" Sage yelped.

"Not until you come with me," the bird said.

"No," said Sage. "Leave me alone."

"Stubborn, silly, sad-faced dog," the bird trilled. "I've been watching you."

The strange bird took flight. He flapped his wings around Sage's ears. He beat at her head until she ran down the hill and across a grassy stretch of land. He chased her toward a stream. Sage jumped over some rocks and splashed on her belly in the water.

"Stubborn, silly, *soggy* dog," the bird whistled. "We're here. Look."

There was a boy standing in the stream near a big buckeye tree. He wore loose trousers, a loose shirt, and a straw hat with a curved brim. A rope of hair trailed down his back.

He was trying to move a big rock from the bottom of the stream with a shovel. He frowned with concentration. His shoulders were bent. It looked like he was carrying a large, invisible weight on his back. He moved awkwardly, like a half-grown puppy.

"He's big for his age," the bird said. "His father and uncle need him to help as much as he can, but he's only a chick. The only one for miles and miles around. I've flown as far as I can to look for another one. His name is Sheng and he's ten years old. He comes from a place far away from here called China."

He flew to the boy named Sheng and landed on his hat. The boy didn't look up.

"Stop that, Choi Hung," Sheng said to the bird. "There could be gold under this rock. I just have to get to it. We have to get as much as we can."

"Brought a dog!" Choi Hung said to Sheng in human words. "Brought a dog!"

Sage had never heard an animal speak like humans spoke!

Sheng looked and saw Sage flopped there in the water. He put his shovel down on the bank of the stream. Sage got to her paws. Sage and the boy watched each other for a moment. Then, very slowly, Sheng raised his hand. Sage tensed her legs. Was he going to throw something at her to make her leave?

Choi Hung flew back to her. He poked Sage on the head.

"Don't keep doing that!" she barked.

"Cowardly, cowering, craven dog!" Choi Hung responded. "You need a friend. He needs a friend. All he thinks about is trying to find enough gold for his family. *Go!*"

Sage took a step toward the boy. He held out his hand, like a paw. She took another step. And another.

When they were close enough to touch, she sniffed his hand. Then she licked it. He tasted like stream water.

"Hello, girl," he said.

It had been a long time since anyone had spoken kindly to Sage. She wagged her tail weakly.

She looked down at the rock in the stream-bed. Sheng needed help.

She pushed at the rock with her front paws.

Sheng grinned. He picked up his shovel and slid it under the rock. Together, they worked it loose.

Sheng turned the rock over. "No gold," he said. His shoulders slumped. He dropped his shovel on the rocks. "But thank you for helping." He ruffled Sage's ears.

"You know, most of my family is gone," he said. "It's just Father and Uncle and me. Most of my friends back home are gone too." He wiped his sleeve over his eyes, but he didn't cry.

"You look like you're all by yourself," he said. "Do you feel lonely and sad too? Maybe you could stay with us. You're the color of gold! You could be Bo-Bo—a little treasure. I bet you'll bring us luck!"

Sage almost shook with hope. *I'll be tough enough this time,* she told herself. *I won't be too soft.*

Sheng lived with his father and Uncle Gwan in a tent just up the hill from the stream.

"Can Bo-Bo stay, Father?" he asked. "I named her after treasure! She can help us find gold!"

Father looked down at her. His eyes were tired. But he smiled. Sage liked the way his braid of dark hair swung over his shoulder in front of his shirt and the way his face crinkled at her.

"I think," said Father, "a boy should have a dog. Dogs make good friends."

"Good friends!" Choi Hung repeated. "Good friends!"

Sage, who was now Bo-Bo, wagged her tail to show him how eager she was to do her part. Sheng's father gave her a handful of warm rice. She gulped it down. A shudder of happiness went through her whole body. Her lonely days wandering over endless hills were over. She would never let anything send her back to that life again.

3
Gold

Three months later Bo-Bo shook the water
from her fur. She bounded up the bank of the
stream with a rock in her mouth. She brought
it to Uncle Gwan. He sat on a rickety wooden
stool with his leg stretched out. He had broken
it months ago and it hadn't healed well. Bo-Bo
set down the rock and then ran back into the

stream for more. She knew that sometimes there were bits of gold in the bigger rocks.

Sheng and his father stood in the water. They both held shallow, wide metal pans in their hands. They scooped rocks and mud from the bottom of the stream with the pans. They sloshed them around and around. The gravel and mud washed over the side with the water. The heavier rocks stayed at the bottom. If Sheng and Father were lucky, some of those rocks would be gold. Over and over they scooped and swished, scooped and swished.

Gold. It was why thousands and thousands of people had come to California. Acorn, who had lived with a miner once, had told Bo-Bo

all about it. A man named James Marshall had found gold at Mr. Sutter's mill. The news had flown across the land like hungry birds. People from all over the country left their homes to come to California to get rich.

Word had spread across the ocean to China, too. It reached Sheng's father and uncle in a place called the Pearl River Delta. They had spent everything they had to take a ship to California.

"But why would they leave?" Bo-Bo had asked Choi Hung the first night she'd spent with the family. She couldn't understand why anyone would leave home if they didn't have to.

"There was something called *war*," Choi

Hung had trilled. "It meant that people came to their village and tried to hurt them. And then there was something called *famine*. That meant there wasn't enough food to eat. That's why Sheng's flock is so small now. After that, people left. Some of them heard there was a place called Gum San, Gold Mountain. They said there was gold just lying on the ground. That if you weren't careful, you'd trip over it! And that if you waded into the water, your shoes would fill up with gold!"

But it wasn't true. Sheng's family had found a few flakes of gold in a part of the stream where no one else was looking for it. They marked it as their claim. That meant that it was their place to look for gold and no one else was allowed to. They worked and worked. But they had to spend half of what they found just on food and supplies. A shovel cost as much as a stove did back home. An egg was as much as a week's worth of food anywhere else.

They couldn't save the other half because of the Foreign Miner's Tax.

Every month Chinese miners had to pay

an extra three dollars to Mr. Smeets, the tax collector. If they didn't, Mr. Smeets would take their claim. They would have nowhere to go. They would starve just like they would have back home.

"But that's not fair!" Bo-Bo had barked to Choi Hung the first time she'd heard of the tax. "Why do they have to pay and other miners don't?"

"Mr. Smeets doesn't care about fair," Choi Hung had answered. "He cares about making money." The bird shook his tail feathers. "He gets some money from the tax. But he gets even more selling the claim if they don't pay."

The tax was due tomorrow, and Bo-Bo didn't know if they had enough. Sheng looked worried. He swished the water faster and faster in the pan. His brow furrowed as he searched for sparkles.

Bo-Bo ran back to the stream and brought another rock to Uncle Gwan. She set it down beside him.

"You're making me dizzy, running back and forth," Choi Hung complained.

"Then don't watch!" Bo-Bo barked at him.

Choi Hung had lived

with the captain of the ship that Sheng's family took on the long trip from China. Uncle Gwan had given the ship's captain his best hat and some salted fish and taken Choi Hung with him. Choi Hung liked California better than the ship. He got seasick.

Uncle Gwan broke open the stone with a hammer. Bo-Bo panted, hoping he'd find something.

"Bad luck, girl," Uncle Gwan said. "No gold."

Bo-Bo pawed through the pieces of rock, hoping Uncle Gwan was wrong.

She heard a branch snap.

4
Mr. Smeets

Sheng and his father waded from the stream. Mr. Smeets never came by just to visit.

"Good evening," he said to Sheng's father and uncle.

His words sounded different from the ones Sheng and his family used. Bo-Bo had learned that some groups of people used one

She woofed. Everyone looked up just as a man stepped out from the trees. He was short and stocky and had a scraggly mustache. He smelled like he wanted something he shouldn't have.

It was Mr. Smeets.

set of words and some used others. Unlike dogs, they couldn't always understand one another. The different ways of speaking were called languages. The one that Mr. Smeets spoke was called English.

Sheng's father answered with the same words. "Good evening, Mr. Smeets."

Mr. Smeets strolled around their little camp. He looked into their rice barrel. He took a drink from their water bucket. He picked up a chisel and put it in his pocket. Bo-Bo growled. "Quiet, girl," Sheng whispered.

"Just wanted to remind you that the tax is due tomorrow," Mr. Smeets said.

Sheng's father nodded at Sheng. Sheng

spoke English better than his father.

"Yes, sir," Sheng said. "We know. Can we help you with anything?"

"Just want to make sure you have enough gold to pay for it," Mr. Smeets said. "I'd hate to see you lose this claim."

"Hah!" Uncle Gwan said under his breath.

"What did you say?" said Mr. Smeets.

"I said, 'Thank you,'" Uncle Gwan said. He smiled. Choi Hung twittered.

Mr. Smeets harrumphed. He sauntered out of camp.

"It's *still* not fair!" Bo-Bo woofed to Choi Hung as soon as Mr. Smeets left.

"Not fair," Choi Hung agreed.

Sheng's father frowned at Uncle Gwan.

"You shouldn't risk making him angry," he said. "You don't know what he'll do. Yuen Kong told me that the white miners in Sheeptown went to the Chinese camp there. They pulled down their tents and broke their equipment.

What they couldn't break they threw in the river. They even cut off their bin." Bo-Bo knew that "bin" was the name for their long braids of hair.

Sheng looked horrified. "But that means they can never go home," he cried out. "They'd be killed for not wearing bin!"

Uncle Gwan frowned right back at Sheng's father. "I say someone needs to throw Mr. Smeets in the river," he said.

"We can't make him angry, Uncle," Sheng said. "We can't lose the claim. It's all we have. I'll work harder, Father."

Father stretched and rubbed the small of his back. "You work hard enough, Sheng."

Bo-Bo stepped on Sheng's foot so he'd look at her.

I'll help you get more gold, she tried to tell him. He looked down at her.

"It's up to me, Bo-Bo," he whispered. "Uncle is hurt and Father can't do everything. I have to get more gold so we can stay on the claim. No matter what it takes."

It was almost dark. Sheng helped Uncle Gwan up from his stool. They made their way back to their camp as darkness fell.

Father weighed the bits of gold they had saved that month.

"Do we have enough for the tax?" Sheng asked. Bo-Bo hated how scared he sounded.

Father smiled. "Yes," he said. "Three dollars exactly. You be careful taking it to town tomorrow. Pay the tax and come straight back home."

Sheng was the one who went into the town of Pickax Flat to pay the tax. He could talk to the men in town better than his father could. And that way, his father could guard their claim.

"Bo-Bo will protect you," Sheng's father said. Bo-Bo didn't know how to tell him she wasn't tough enough to protect anyone.

They had their supper of rice and green squash. Bo-Bo ate hers faster than anyone else. Then they ducked into the simple canvas tent. Sheng and his father sat on their bedrolls. Uncle Gwan sat on the only stool. Bo-Bo

snuggled up to Sheng with her head on his lap.

Uncle Gwan began to talk. Every night he told them stories he'd heard from the sailors on their boat, who heard them from the people they took back and forth to Gold Mountain. Or sometimes he made them up himself. Uncle Gwan told of ghosts who haunted old gold claims and pirates who boarded ships carrying gold across the ocean. Then he would sing songs.

"I have been in Gold Mountain for so long,

But my family and home stay forever in my heart."

That night, he told his favorite story: "The Story of Crooked Cave."

"There was once a prospector," he began as he always did, "who struck it rich. But he made enemies who wanted his gold. So he hid it deep in a cave. There was so much gold there that it would take a hundred mules to carry it. The prospector made a map so he could find it again. He put his mark on the map. It was a rain cloud over a mountain. One stormy night he wandered into the hills. The legend says he was struck by lightning or fell into a deep canyon. But he was never heard from again.

"The cave is high up in the hills," Uncle

Gwan said. "Nobody knows exactly where. And no one has ever found the map. I almost found the cave once. I was just over near—"

"Enough," Father said. "I wish you'd stop telling that story. You broke your leg looking for that cave!"

Uncle Gwan stopped talking. "It's only a story," he said. But he winked at Sheng.

"Only a story!" Choi Hung repeated.

Bo-Bo liked the stories and songs. But often when Uncle Gwan had finished, she felt sadness settle on their tent.

Sheng pulled her close and whispered to her. "I miss home. Before the war, when we walked into our house at night, we could smell a big pot of rice cooking. It doesn't smell the same here. I wish we'd never had to leave. I wish we had a big pot of rice. I wish we had enough gold to never worry about the tax again. I wish Crooked Cave was real."

5
Pickax Flat

The early-morning sky was already bright above Pickax Flat. Only a few small white clouds floated by. Bo-Bo and Sheng had left home when it was still dark. The town stood on level ground among the hills. The road under Bo-Bo's paws changed from dust and pebbles to hard-packed dirt.

"Hey, watch where you're going!" some-one neighed. A hoof clopped down right next to Bo-Bo's paw! "Get out from underfoot," said the horse who had nearly flattened her into a flapjack.

"Sorry," Bo-Bo woofed. The horse had already stomped on, led by a man in a tall hat.

There was so much going on in town, Bo-Bo never knew where to look. Men bustled in and out of the low buildings. There was a saloon with a rooming house next to it, a general store, and a blacksmith.

Halfway down the street, right in the middle of the road, stood a wagon. A man with a bushy, light brown beard walked back and forth in front of it. He yelled and waved his arms.

"Come see the best show this side of the Sierra mountains!" he shouted. "Only twenty-five cents to see the greatest fight of the year!"

Bo-Bo stared. In a cage on the wagon was a grizzly bear. It was bigger than Father and Uncle Gwan put together. It pushed its muzzle through the bars and snarled. Bo-Bo jumped. Men scurried back from the cage.

Bo-Bo pressed up against Sheng's leg. Sheng kept one hand curled around the little leather bag of gold dust in his pocket. Bo-Bo knew he hated going to town and talking to Mr. Smeets.

Mr. Smeets collected taxes from a small desk in the general store. A line of men waited outside. They were all from China, like Sheng and his family. Sheng took a deep breath and joined them. He was the only boy there.

The door to the store burst open. A Chinese man stumbled out. Mr. Smeets strode out after him.

"I don't care why you can't pay the tax!" Mr. Smeets said. "You don't pay the three dollars, you don't keep your claim."

"Just a few more days," the man pleaded. Like all the Chinese miners, he spoke English to Mr. Smeets.

"The tax is due *now*," Mr. Smeets said.

"Get out of here. Or else."

He shoved the man hard and the man stumbled again. The man tried to keep his head up. He walked down the street and out of town.

Mr. Smeets looked at everyone in line.

"I think I'll have my break-fast," he said. "You

foreigners don't mind waiting, do you?" He gave them all a nasty grin. Bo-Bo could feel Sheng tense. She worked hard not to growl. But she could glare.

"I think I'll have myself some Hangtown fry," Mr. Smeets said. Bo-Bo's mouth watered. Hangtown fry was made of bacon, oysters, and eggs. It was so expensive, she knew she'd never get to taste it.

Mr. Smeets started to saunter across the street. He didn't see Bo-Bo. He tripped right over her.

"What the—?!" he yelled. He tried to kick her but missed. A large piece of paper fell out of his jacket. He snatched it quickly from the ground. He looked around suspiciously.

"Keep this animal away from me!" he said. He straightened his jacket and walked toward the saloon.

Sheng crouched down and put his arm around Bo-Bo. "Sorry, girl," he said softly. She rubbed his cheek with her nose. It wasn't his fault.

Bo-Bo was thirsty. She saw a water trough for horses down the street.

But the trough was right near the bear's wagon.

It's okay, she told herself. *That bear's in a cage. It can't hurt me.*

She padded to the trough and nosed her

way between the horses. She stood on her hind legs and put her paws on the edge of the trough. She drank. It was delicious.

"That man will starve to death for sure," muttered the horse who had almost stepped on Bo-Bo.

"Yep," the stallion next to her neighed. "No claim, no gold, no nothing."

The horses seemed to know a lot about

what happened in town. Bo-Bo swallowed a big slurp of water.

"Why do they care if people come from China?" she asked the mare. "What difference does it make?"

"Who knows," the mare answered. "But they do care. They get upset when someone looks different, or talks differently, or eats different food. And then there's the gold. Makes people want more and more, and makes them hate each other. Seems like nonsense to me, but that's people for you."

Bo-Bo heard someone shouting.

It was the bearded man in front of the wagon. "Watch the most spectacular bear fight you have ever seen!" he cried. "This freshly caught grizzly pitted against the famous bull, Columbia! The ferocious bull arrives first thing tomorrow morning!"

The cage was a box with heavy bars on all sides. There was no way the bear could smash it open. She paced back and forth as much as she could in the small space. Every time she tried to turn around, she had to shuffle awkwardly. *How terrible*, thought Bo-Bo.

"Not recently fed or watered!" cried the man with the brown beard. He walked away from the wagon to some men farther down the street. "She's ready to fight!"

Bo-Bo was afraid of bears. All smart animals were. But to keep one hungry and thirsty so she would fight? And in a cage? That was just wrong.

The grizzly stopped pacing. She stared at Bo-Bo. Bo-Bo froze. The bear grunted, "Come here, dog."

6
Resilience

Bo-Bo looked behind her to see what dog the bear was talking to.

"You!" said the bear.

"Me?"

"You!"

Bo-Bo ducked under the trough and walked up to the cage. The grizzly snuffled quietly at her. Each of the bear's paws was as big as Bo-Bo's head, and each of her claws was as big as one of Bo-Bo's paws.

"Do you know the grove of willows near a narrow part of the stream?" She jerked her head toward the far side of town.

"Yes," said Bo-Bo slowly.

The bear sat on her haunches. She looked more sad than fierce. Her shoulders drooped and her snout pointed miserably at the ground.

"That's where they got me yesterday," she grunted. Underneath her gruff voice, she suddenly seemed to choke back whimpers. "But they didn't get my cub!"

"Your *cub*?" said Bo-Bo.

"He's all alone . . ."

"What happened?" Bo-Bo asked.

"They had a bear trap with some nice juicy fish." She snuffled again. "My cub will try to follow me, and they might get him, too. Can you try to get a message to him when you leave town? That he should stay away from the camps no matter how hun-

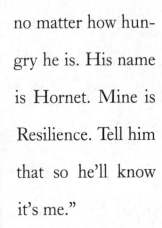

gry he is. His name is Hornet. Mine is Resilience. Tell him that so he'll know it's me."

"I'll try!" Bo-Bo woofed.

"Bo-Bo!" Sheng called. "Get away from that bear! Come here, girl!"

The bear whimpered. Bo-Bo wished she could make her feel better. She looked at the lock on the cage.

It was a latch with a strong metal pin that slid down to fit into a metal groove. There was a metal bar across it. It wasn't one of those locks that needed a key.

She'd seen a latch like this on a chicken coop her old pack had raided.

Out there wandering in the hills was a lonely bear cub, far away from his mother. *Maybe he's curled up in a hollow,* Bo-Bo thought. *Maybe he doesn't even want to eat.* She knew how that felt.

She looked around quickly. Nobody but Sheng was watching her. She stood on her hind legs and put her front paws up on the cage.

Carefully, she lifted the latch with her nose. She couldn't quite keep it high enough. But Resilience saw what she was doing.

"Oh, dog!" she grunted. "Here, I can help." She stuck one sharp claw through the bars. It was just enough to hold the latch up. Bo-Bo nosed open the metal bar.

The cage door swung open.

"Bo-Bo!" Sheng shouted. "Get out of the way!"

Resilience leaped from the cage.

"Thank you," the bear rumbled. She let out a great roar and bounded down the street.

Everything seemed to happen at once. A man hollered, "That bear's loose! *Run!*" Someone screamed. Men ducked into buildings and dove under wagons. Resilience

paused for just an instant to drink from the water trough. The horses reared up and galloped through the blacksmith's shop, sending tools flying. Gunfire rang out. Someone bellowed, "Don't you dare shoot my investment!"

The voice belonged to Mr. Smeets. He charged toward the man who had fired, grabbed his gun, and threw it to the ground. "That bear's mine! Don't you *ever* risk something that belongs to me!"

Bo-Bo didn't understand. How could someone own a bear? Resilience belonged to herself.

Resilience bounded toward the hills. Even

though the trees and boulders were sparse, she was soon lost among them.

She's free, Bo-Bo thought. *Her cub will be safe.*

Sheng ran toward Bo-Bo. "Are you all right, girl?" he asked. She licked his hand and thumped her tail to show him she was. Then he knelt down next to her. "Oh, Bo-Bo," he said in her ear in a very different kind of voice. "What have you done?"

7
Gone Gold

Mr. Smeets stood in the middle of the road.
His fists were clenched.

"Who let my bear out?" he said. "Who did it?"

"I saw it all, Bill," said the man who had fired the gun. "It was that dog there!"

He pointed at Bo-Bo. She lowered her ears.

"I saw it too," a third man said. "Used her nose and opened up the latch. Not a bad trick."

"Well, whose flea-bitten mongrel is that?" demanded Mr. Smeets.

Bo-Bo prickled. "I am *not* flea-bitten!" she barked.

"She belongs to that foreign boy!" the man with the gun said. He pointed at Sheng.

When he said the word "foreign," his voice turned nasty. Sheng flinched. Bo-Bo started to shake. *Foreign!* There was that word again. Didn't they know Sheng couldn't go home? Like she couldn't go back to her old pack!

"Get him!" Mr. Smeets ordered. "And the mutt."

Two of the men grabbed Sheng. Someone seized Bo-Bo by the scruff of her neck. She struggled, but the man who held her was too strong. Sheng yelled. Bo-Bo growled. A second man grabbed her.

Before she knew it, the men had dragged them behind the saloon. They pinned Sheng against the wall by his shoulders. Two men still held Bo-Bo by the neck fur.

"Let him go!" she growled.

Mr. Smeets leaned over Sheng.

"My bear was worth

two hundred dollars, boy," he said. "And your dog let her go! Did you tell her to do it?"

Sheng shook his head fast. Mr. Smeets put his face right next to Sheng's.

"You owe me two hundred dollars!" he said. "In gold!"

"I . . . I don't have two hundred dollars," Sheng said. "Not in gold, or any other way."

"See how much he has, Pete," Mr. Smeets ordered.

The men held Sheng's arms fast. Sheng kicked and struggled. His feet came off the ground. Bo-Bo barked desperately. The man named Pete turned out Sheng's pockets. He found the leather bag of gold dust. He tossed it in his hand and caught it. "Only about three dollars here, I'd say."

"That's our gold for the tax!" Sheng protested.

"Not anymore," Mr. Smeets said.

"That's not fair!" Sheng shouted.

"Fair?" said Pete. "What's not fair is you

people coming over and taking our gold. You should go back to where you came from." He put the bag of gold dust into his pocket. "We'll take this for your tax. And you still owe Mr. Smeets two hundred dollars."

Sheng went limp. "How am I going to get two hundred dollars?" he whispered. It seemed to Bo-Bo that the fight had gone out of him.

Mr. Smeets smiled. "Well, your father's claim should just about cover it," he said.

Sheng's eyes widened. "No," he mouthed.

We can't lose the claim! Bo-Bo thought.

"But tell you what," Mr. Smeets went on. "It's your lucky day. It so happens I've got a thing or two to do outside town first. How much is gold selling for today, Pete?" he asked.

"Twenty dollars and sixteen cents an ounce," Pete said, grinning.

"Two hundred dollars is about ten ounces of gold," Mr. Smeets said. "I'm a forgiving man. I'll make you a deal. If you bring me ten ounces of gold by sundown, I'll forget all about this. If not, I'll take your father's claim and we'll call it even. Sound fair to you, Pete?"

"Sounds fair to me," Pete answered.

Mr. Smeets nodded at the two men who were holding Sheng. They let him go.

"Better get started!" he called. He sauntered away.

The men holding Bo-Bo let go of her, too. She ran to Sheng. The men walked away, laughing.

Sheng's face twisted with misery and anger. "Where could I ever find that much gold all at once?" he whispered. "The most we've ever found is one ounce in a whole month! Why can Mr. Smeets just do that to us?" He kicked the wall.

A crow cawed overhead. Sheng looked up at it and blinked hard. Bo-Bo could tell he was trying not to cry.

"You're a good dog, Bo-Bo," he said. "I know you are. But why did you do that? How can I even go home to Father and Uncle? I

don't know anywhere I could get that gold! Not in one day!"

He sat down against the wall and stared at the ground.

Gold again. Those pebbles and bits of rock that always seemed to be so important. And Sheng needed enough gold to be worth two hundred of those things called "dollars." Before sundown.

I did it again, thought Bo-Bo. *I was too soft, just like Thunder said.* Sheng and his family were going to lose everything they had worked so hard for. All because she had felt sorry for a bear. They would have nowhere to go. They would starve.

And it was all her fault.

8
The Ringtail

Bo-Bo nudged Sheng's arm. Would he send her away like Thunder had? *You're weak,* said a voice in her head. *Soft.*

Sheng raised his head.

"Give me a little while, Bo-Bo," he said.

She whimpered. She wished Choi Hung was there.

He'd tell her to stop feeling sorry for herself. He'd call her a moping mutt.

Sheng said, "I have to figure out what to do."

Oh no you don't, thought Bo-Bo. *I will!*

She would fix everything. She had to find a way.

"Hey. Dog. Cage-opening dog."

Bo-Bo looked up. An animal crouched in the shade beneath the overhang of the saloon roof. She looked like a cross between a weasel and a cat. Her ears were as big as a fox's, and her bushy tail was striped like a raccoon's. It was longer than the whole rest of her. Bo-Bo knew what she was. She had seen one before, in the camp where Thunder was shot. The animal was called a ringtail, and miners kept them to eat mice and bugs.

"I saw you rescue that bear," the ringtail said. "That was bold." That surprised Bo-Bo. *I'm not bold*, she thought.

"Listen," the ringtail said. "I know how you can get enough gold to pay for twenty bears. Get me out of here too, and I'll show you."

Bo-Bo saw now

that there was a leather collar around the ring-tail's neck. It was attached to a chain that went through a small hole high in the wall and then into the saloon.

Bo-Bo tried to be tough.

"How could you possibly help us?" she said. She moved a little away from Sheng.

The ringtail twitched her big ears. "Mr. Smeets keeps me chained up here," she squeaked at Bo-Bo. "It's his saloon, you know. He charges people to see me when he doesn't have a bear or a bull. If you can free me, I'll give you something called a *map*."

"What good would that do?" said Bo-Bo. She hoped she was still being tough.

"Plenty," answered the ringtail. "And your boy will know how to read it. It shows the way to a cave near here. There's so much gold hidden there, it would take a hundred mules to carry it."

A hundred mules. That was exactly what Uncle Gwan had said. "Crooked Cave?!" Bo-Bo woofed. "You have a map to Crooked Cave? How?"

"I took it from Mr. Smeets. I hate Mr. Smeets. He captured me and keeps me as part of his show. He doesn't even give me a nice box to keep the sun off me during the day. I don't like being awake during the day." She paused.

"He locks me in his study at night to catch mice. Sometimes I let them get away."

"I hate Mr. Smeets too," Bo-Bo said. She looked at Sheng. He had buried his head in his hands.

"Well," said the ringtail. "Mr. Smeets got this map last night. Found it hidden on some claim he stole. I heard him say it's the way to Crooked Cave. He put it high up on a shelf. I stole it, like he stole me. And I hid it in the study. Free me, and it's yours."

"Give me the map and then I'll let you go," Bo-Bo said.

"Can't do it," the ringtail said. "I don't trust

anyone when there's gold involved. Besides, I can't get to it from here. But I always pay my debts. Always."

Bo-Bo didn't know whether to trust the ringtail. But if she was telling the truth, they could pay for the bear. They could stay on the claim.

"All right," she said. "What do I do?"

"This chain runs inside the saloon. It's attached to a stake dug into the floor. Dig out the stake. I'll do the rest."

Bo-Bo looked around. No one else was there. Even Sheng wasn't watching her. He didn't seem able to move.

"I'll do it," she said.

She padded around the building and under the door into the saloon.

9
The Map

The room was noisy and smoky. Men were drinking coffee or playing cards or talking at tables. Another man was serving them. There were even some chickens strutting around. Bo-Bo's mouth watered, but she ignored them. No one looked when she slunk by.

She saw the chain snaking across the floor.

She followed it to a dark corner of the room. There it was hooked to a narrow wooden stake.

The dirt floor of the saloon was hard. Bo-Bo dug as quickly as she could. The stake had just come out of the ground when—

Squawk!

A chicken had seen her.

"Dog! Dog!" the chicken squawked. In a second all the chickens were in a panic. "Dog! Dog!" they all cried. They fluttered up onto tables and chairs to get as far away from Bo-Bo as they could.

One of the men threw down his cards. "What's going on?!"

"That's the mutt who caused all the trouble!" another said. "Let's get her! I'll bet we could get another three dollars for her!"

He was one of the men who had shoved Sheng and taken his money. A wave of anger washed over Bo-Bo.

"Just try it!" she woofed.

They moved in on her.

Bo-Bo crouched. She waited until they were almost on top of her. Then she ran between the two men. They tried to grab her and bumped into each other instead.

The whole saloon saw her now. Three more men ran at her. She ran between one man's legs. He tried to grab her but fell on his rump.

Another one landed right on top of him. The man who had fallen swung a fist at the man who landed on him. He missed and hit a man behind him, who swung back. In half a minute everyone in the saloon was fighting.

Bo-Bo darted between everyone's feet. The chain rippled across the floor and up the wall. The ringtail must be pulling on it.

Bo-Bo ran toward the saloon door. A wonderful smell drifted under her nose. There on a table was a plate with a bit of Hangtown fry on it. Mr. Smeets's leftovers! Bo-Bo knew she'd never get a chance to try that expensive Hangtown fry again. She gulped it down, then bolted out of the saloon.

The ringtail waited at the back of the building. She had jumped down from her perch. Sheng had stood up and was calling Bo-Bo.

"Where'd you go?" he asked. "Did you get into more trouble?" They could hear the banging and crashing of the fight inside the saloon. Sheng's question hurt Bo-Bo's feelings, but she couldn't stop to think about that now. She had to make sure the ringtail kept her end of the bargain.

"Where's the map?" she woofed.

"Hold your horses!" the ringtail said. She ran to the rooming house next to the saloon and jumped into a window. The chain and the stake trailed behind her. She came back with a roll of tattered canvas in her mouth. It was crumbling around the edges. She dropped it next to Bo-Bo.

"Good luck!" the ringtail said. She began to scurry away. The chain clanked behind her.

"Wait!" Bo-Bo called. "You're not going to get far that way. Stay still."

The ringtail stopped. She kept a front paw raised, ready to run.

Bo-Bo sniffed at the chain and collar. The collar was held together by a simple buckle at the back of the ringtail's neck. There was no way the ringtail could have reached it.

"Don't bite me," she ordered. She took the piece of leather that went through the buckle in her teeth and pulled at it until the collar loosened. The ringtail put a front paw on each side of it and pushed it over her head. She started to run away. Then she stopped.

"You didn't have to do that," she said. "You could have just taken the map and left. I won't forget." Then she darted away.

Bo-Bo ran back to Sheng. He had unrolled the map and was staring at it.

"This is . . . this is . . ." It sounded like he was almost afraid to say it. "Look! This is

the map to Crooked Cave!" He traced some lines on it with his finger. "It's faded, but I can see that rain cloud over a mountain! Just like Uncle Gwan said!" He shook his head in disbelief.

Bo-Bo sniffed the map.

"Look!"

All Bo-Bo saw were some marks on the canvas. But they meant something to Sheng.

"This drawing of buildings, this must

be Pickax Flat, right where we are now," he said. "And those are the hills to the east." He looked toward the hills that loomed in the distance.

"So we leave town to the north; then we go to the east to some big stones shaped like four fingers sticking up in the air, near these three pine trees. From there we cross a river and head downstream. Then we cross a canyon—I think that must be Buzzard Canyon. I've heard miners talk about that—see the drawing of the buzzard? And then at this X is a cave—Crooked Cave! This is where the prospector left all his gold!"

He whooped. He picked up Bo-Bo's front paws and danced around with her. She opened her mouth in a big grin and let her tongue hang out. A lump in her chest loosened. "We're going to be all right, Bo-Bo!" Sheng said.

He dropped her paws. "What was that ringtail doing with this?" he wondered. He rolled up the map and put it in his pocket. Someone in the saloon was yelling. It sounded like Mr. Smeets shouting at everyone not to break his property.

"We'd better get out of here," Sheng said. "Come on, Bo-Bo! Let's show those crooks how much gold we can get!"

10
Rattlesnake Rock

They left the town behind, but Bo-Bo's anger stayed with her. She was angry with the men who took Sheng's money. Angry with Mr. Smeets for being so greedy. Most of all, she was angry with herself for letting it all happen.

Determination settled on her like a second layer of fur. She wouldn't let her own weakness cost Sheng and his family everything. This time, she'd make up for her mistake.

They walked and walked and then they walked some more. Bo-Bo was thirsty again. Sheng shook his canteen. It was almost empty.

"The air is so dry here!" he said. "It makes your throat feel like tree bark. Back home it's hot, but at least the air isn't full of dust." He poured some water into his palm for Bo-Bo. She lapped it up. Sheng drank the rest.

"We'll have to get more soon," he said.

He unrolled the map. He pointed to something on it. "We'll get some when we get to this river." It just looked like a wavy line to Bo-Bo, but somehow Sheng knew it meant there was a river there.

"But first we need those rocks near the pine trees," he said. He looked up and pointed at two hills, one to the left, one to the right. "They could be over either of those hills," he said. "But I can't tell which one from the map. It shows a lot of hills."

Pine trees. Bo-Bo couldn't read a map, but she knew pine trees when she smelled them. Their sweet, sharp scent floated toward her on the breeze. She lifted her nose to the air.

She followed the scent, walking a few paces toward the hill on the left. But Sheng kept staring at the map. She tugged on his shirt. He just frowned and looked up at the hills again.

Bo-Bo had to get him to follow her. She grabbed the canteen from his grip and ran.

"Bo-Bo!" Sheng shouted. "Come back here! I need that!"

Bo-Bo dashed up the hill toward the scent. Sheng raced after her.

When she reached the top, she looked down. There it was! A cluster of rocks, like four fingers pointing straight up into the sky.

Sheng came panting behind her.

"What were you thinking?" he said. He took the canteen from her. Then he looked down the hill. His eyes widened in surprise. "It's the rocks! Surrounded by trees! It's right there. That's lucky." Bo-Bo wagged her tail.

Sheng ran down the hill. Bo-Bo followed. When they reached the trees, Sheng leaned against one of the rocks, where there was a little shade.

"The map says the river is downhill and to the south," he said. "We cross it at a big oak tree. There's a bridge there." He was still breathing hard. It was getting very hot. He shook the empty canteen and licked his dry lips.

"The white miners don't have to pay three dollars a month just to keep their claims," he grumbled. "None of them would ever have to be out here frying like an egg."

Bo-Bo had never heard Sheng talk like that before.

Rattle Rattle Rattle!

Bo-Bo knew what that sound was. A snake was coiled up next to a hole under the rock. Right by her left paw! Its flat, triangular head was lowered. Its small eyes glared. Its tail was lifted high above the rest of it. *Rattle!*

Sheng gasped. Bo-Bo scooched backward until her rump was next to Sheng.

Rattle Rattle Rattle! That sound came from behind them. It was another snake.

Rattle Rattle! Another one.

Bo-Bo knew what you were supposed to do around rattlers. Don't disturb them, and back away slowly.

But the snakes were already disturbed. And she and Sheng couldn't back up any farther.

The snakes hissed. Sheng reached up toward the tree above him. He grasped a branch and snapped it off. He held it up, ready for a fight.

Bo-Bo snuffled quietly so she wouldn't startle the snakes. "We don't mean any harm," she told the one closest to her. It drew back its head.

"Then why are you here?" the snake said. "With one of those gold hunters?" She bobbed her head toward Sheng. "Men come here and take everything. They dig up our dens. This is *our* home. *They* stole it."

"We don't want anything!" Bo-Bo barked. "We just—"

The snake leaped at her. Sheng shouted and swung his stick. Bo-Bo jumped straight into the air. She landed in a crouch and grabbed the snake behind its head. She threw it as far as she could. It landed with a hiss and slid back toward them. Another snake moved in. Then another. Suddenly it seemed like the entire ground around the rock was alive with snakes.

Bo-Bo's fury returned. They were threatening Sheng! Like the men in town had. Like Mr. Smeets had. Her whole body got hot, and she growled a deeper growl than she had ever growled before.

She pounced among the snakes.

Sheng ran forward with his stick. Bo-Bo couldn't let him be bitten. She yelped and threw another snake. Two more closed in on her.

THWACK! A rock landed between the two snakes. There was a blur of bright colors and sharp talons and a beak.

"Choi Hung!" cried Sheng.

The bird dove down and flew up and then dove down again. Sheng swung his stick. Bo-Bo barked and growled. The snakes began to slither away, into crevices and holes. Bo-Bo snatched one behind its head.

I can crush you right now, she thought. *That's what Thunder would do.*

The snake flopped around desperately, trying to escape her jaws.

Suddenly, Bo-Bo was ashamed. The snake was now all alone against her, Sheng, and

Choi Hung. It was just trying to take care of its home. Just like she was trying to take care of Sheng and the claim. She didn't want to be like the men in town or Mr. Smeets.

She let the snake go. It hissed in relief and slid away.

Choi Hung fluttered to Sheng's shoulder.

"Choi Hung, what are you doing here?" Sheng asked, stroking Choi Hung's feathers.

"Dim, dust-brained dog!" Choi Hung said to Bo-Bo. "Don't you know better than to play with rattlesnakes?"

Bo-Bo ignored this. "What *are* you doing here?" she asked.

"I heard from a vulture, who heard from

a hawk, who heard from a crow that you were in trouble." He cocked his head from side to side. "Where are you going?"

"Crooked Cave!" Bo-Bo answered. She quickly told Choi Hung what had happened in town. "Sheng has the map Uncle Gwan talked about! We're going to find the gold there!"

"Well, it's about time!" Choi Hung squawked.

Sheng was standing still, staring back toward town. "You know what?" he said. "It's not fair that we have to pay this stupid tax. It's not fair that Mr. Smeets and those awful men stole our gold. I'm starting to think maybe . . ."

Maybe what? Bo-Bo wondered.

Sheng shook his head. "But we don't have a choice," he said. "Come on, you two. Let's get to that bridge."

11
The River

Sheng stood at the river. He stared at the bridge. It was nothing more than some logs and branches tied together. Underneath it, the water rushed and foamed.

Choi Hung bobbed on Sheng's shoulder.

"Not a bridge!" he squawked. "Not a bridge!"

Sheng filled his canteen with water while Bo-Bo drank. Then he took a deep breath. He stepped gingerly onto the makeshift bridge. Bo-Bo stayed right by his side. Sheng went down on all fours. *I don't know how they balance at all on only two legs,* Bo-Bo thought.

Sheng crawled forward. Every time he seemed to be making progress, the water splashed over him and almost knocked him

off the logs. Choi Hung spread his wings and held tighter to Sheng. Little by little, they all inched their way across.

"Almost there!" Choi Hung called. "Almost there!"

Sheng reached for the slippery bunch of branches ahead of him. As soon as he put his weight on them, they came loose and rushed downriver. The rope tying them together had rotted away! Sheng gasped. Now there was a wide gap in the bridge.

I'll help him! Bo-Bo thought. If she jumped over the gap to the next set of branches, Sheng could grab on to her and pull himself across. She leaped.

She landed with a thump and a *CRACK*. The wood beneath her broke. She fell into the river.

"Bo-Bo!" Sheng shouted.

The water swirled over her head. She swallowed a stomachful of river. She came up and gulped air. She paddled hard to keep her head above water.

Sheng was beside her. He had jumped in after her! The water was too deep for her to stand up in—could Sheng? One look at his face and she knew he couldn't. He was paddling desperately. This wasn't like the stream on the claim. It was strong and fast.

Bo-Bo tried to swim back to the bridge.

But the current was too strong. Beside her, Sheng spat up water. He tried to get back to the bridge too. His eyes were wide.

Choi Hung soared above them.

"I'll be back!" he squawked. He flew downstream. He flapped his wings harder than Bo-Bo had ever seen him flap. His last shriek as he headed downstream was, "Don't fight! Let the river carry you!"

Carry me? thought Bo-Bo. But she would try anything.

She stopped struggling. As soon as she stopped battling the current, it was much easier for her to stay afloat.

But she was floating away from Sheng. He

 was still fighting to get to the bridge. He slipped under the water, then came back up, and then went under again. She swam as hard as she could to get closer to him.

"Bo-Bo!" he coughed.

His hand grabbed her fur. It gave him just enough breathing space to see what she was doing. She saw him relax and give in to the river. If they could find someplace to get out, they could make it. It needed to be soon. Bo-Bo could see how exhausted Sheng was. She was too.

There! A speck far away in the sky! It got closer and closer!

"Choi Hung!" gulped Bo-Bo. "Where have you been?!"

"Quiet, dog," screeched Choi Hung, circling. "I found a place for you two to get out of this rolling river!"

Bo-Bo kept quiet, although all she wanted to do was bark out, "WHERE?"

Choi Hung said, "Around two more curves, there's an old tree stump. It looks like an angry bobcat. There's some flat land jutting out into the river. Get out there. Don't get swept past it. After that the bank is too steep. You'll keep floating forever."

"Which side?" Bo-Bo gasped.

"That one," Choi Hung said, dipping his wing.

Sheng floated on his belly, swimming like a frog. A frog that kept coughing up water. Bo-Bo tried to paddle back to him but only got another mouthful of water.

"Keep swimming, dog!" Choi Hung trilled.

The water carried them down, down, down the river.

"There it is! There it is!" Choi Hung

squawked in human words. Bo-Bo saw it too.
A big tree trunk with knots that looked like
eyes, twigs that looked like a bobcat's ears,
and a hole near the bottom that looked like an
angry mouth.

She hurled herself against the stump,
catching her paws between two roots. She
hauled herself out of the
water. Sheng tried
to clamber up
after her. But
the current

started to carry him away. His hat floated downriver. Bo-Bo grabbed his shirt in her mouth. Choi Hung grabbed his long braid. They pulled him up onto shore.

Sheng lay on the ground, coughing and spluttering. Finally he sat up. "Thanks!" he said.

He looked around. "I think that river did us a favor." He coughed. "We needed to go a long way down the bank. I think this is just where we need to be!"

Bo-Bo would have wagged her wet tail, but she couldn't bring herself to. Because she knew exactly where they were.

There was no mistaking it. The scent of

scrub grass and manzanita. The gently rolling hills she could see through the trees. And the stump. From this side, it didn't look like a bobcat.

The twigs looked like rabbit ears, and there was a big knot at the bottom like a fluffy tail. It was Jackrabbit Stump.

She was in her old territory.

"Now let's find that canyon," Sheng said. "We walk out of these woods across a plain and up the hill."

Scrub Hill, thought Bo-Bo.

Sheng reached into his pocket. His face fell.

"The map!" he cried.

He ran back to the edge of the river. Bo-Bo grabbed the leg of his pants in case he tried to jump in. He gazed desperately at the foaming water.

But the map was gone.

12
Buzzard Canyon

"*I don't have that whole map memorized,*" Sheng cried. "I'm not sure how to get to the canyon from here."

But Bo-Bo was.

There was only one canyon that it could be. But if Thunder found out she was back . . .

Stay out of our territory, she'd said.

They couldn't stop now. The sun slanted through the trees. It was getting lower in the sky. They had to hurry.

She set off toward the canyon she'd crossed every time the pack hunted ground squirrels.

"You're looking sure of yourself," said Choi Hung.

"The place Sheng calls Buzzard Canyon— I know where it is," said Bo-Bo.

"You don't sound happy about it!" Choi Hung trilled.

Bo-Bo wasn't. Buzzard Canyon was just below Scrub Hill.

If she was lucky, they could get across the

canyon quickly, before anyone even knew they were there.

If I'm lucky, she said to herself. She started walking. She looked back to make sure Sheng was keeping up.

"Wait, Bo-Bo!" called Sheng. "We don't have the map!"

"That doesn't matter!" she barked, even though she knew he wouldn't understand.

Sheng stood with his arms folded. "Stay, Bo-Bo!" he ordered. "We can't just wander off. We'll get lost!"

"Lost!" Choi Hung whistled. He flew between Bo-Bo and Sheng. "Lost!"

"Would you just help?" Bo-Bo said. She snapped at the air near Choi Hung. "I know what I'm doing."

Choi Hung looked at her in surprise. She'd never snapped at him before.

"Mulish, meandering mutt," he said. But he fluttered around Sheng's shoulders.

"Follow the dog," he squawked to Sheng. "Follow the dog!"

"What?" said Sheng.

Bo-Bo started uphill toward the canyon. This time, Sheng and Choi Hung followed.

There was only one safe way across Buzzard Canyon. Bo-Bo knew it well. It was where some scraggly grass and bright flowers held down the slippery dirt. There were stones Sheng could use as handholds. Bo-Bo would take him across that way.

When they reached the canyon, she bounded quickly to the edge, to show Sheng the way down.

It wasn't there anymore.

Everything below had changed. There was only a sheer drop down. There must have been a rockslide. The bottom of the canyon was covered with sharp boulders and rocks.

Bo-Bo looked back at Sheng. He was running toward her.

"Careful, Bo-Bo!" he called. "Don't fall!"

"Don't fall!" Choi Hung squawked. Then he saw that Bo-Bo had stopped.

"What's wrong?" the bird trilled.

Bo-Bo started to answer. Then the fur on her back rose. Her ears shot straight up.

The rockslide wasn't the only problem.

Familiar scents wafted past her nose over the warm air. Scents she knew very, very well.

To her right, on the ridge at the top of Scrub Hill, dogs began to gather. They looked like birds on a branch. One of them was limping.

Bo-Bo looked up at her old pack.

Thunder stared straight down at her. Even from this distance, her stiff body told Bo-Bo she was angry. Very angry.

Thunder bounded down from the ridge. The pack followed.

Sheng was right behind Bo-Bo now. She could feel him tensing as the dogs approached.

Thunder stopped several paces away. The pack gathered behind her. Bo-Bo couldn't help looking at Acorn. Acorn looked away.

But Thunder stared Bo-Bo right in the eye.

"I told you that if you ever came near

Scrub Hill again, you'd be sorry. You should have listened."

Choi Hung clicked his beak angrily. Bo-Bo crouched. She had to get Sheng away from Thunder. But Sheng crouched down next to her and put his arm over her neck.

Juniper said low, "She's got a person with her. We don't harm people."

"I'll get her away from him," growled Thunder. She didn't take her eyes off Bo-Bo. "Then I'll deal with her."

Bo-Bo started to step away from Sheng. At least he'd be safe. But Sheng reached out to gather her closer to him.

"I don't think that's going to work,"

Juniper woofed. "He doesn't look like he's going anywhere."

"She's not worth it, Thunder," piped up Acorn. "You know how people are. If they even *think* we'd harm one of them, they'd send their whole pack out after us. With those things they call guns."

Thunder ignored him. She bared her teeth and stalked toward Bo-Bo.

Sheng squeezed Bo-Bo tight. His hand searched the ground around him. It closed on a sharp stone about the size of Bo-Bo's paw.

Thunder growled more loudly than before.

"Get back!" Sheng said. He lifted up the stone. "She's my family."

"Better listen, huffy, haughty hound," Choi Hung squawked.

"He has good aim," Bo-Bo warned.

Thunder woofed a mean laugh. "Ha! Your boy's as weak as you are!" she said to Bo-Bo.

Sheng? Weak?

"You're wrong!" Bo-Bo almost roared. "It's not weak to care what happens to other creatures, and to help them! It's not weak to be kind!" She curled her lip. "You stay away from him, Thunder. He's my pack now."

Acorn looked from Bo-Bo to Thunder and back again. His tail twitched.

"Don't bother with them, Thunder. The pack is more important," he said.

Thunder finally broke her stare at Bo-Bo.

"For the pack," she barked gruffly. "I won't risk the pack." Then she snarled at Bo-Bo, "But you get out of here now. If I ever see or smell you here again, I won't care if you've got a boy with you or not. Or a stupid pigeon."

"Hey!" squawked Choi Hung.

The pack walked past Bo-Bo. Sheng watched. He didn't move.

Acorn trailed behind, the last to go. He passed close enough to Bo-Bo to touch noses, although he didn't.

As he went by, he woofed very low, "If you're trying to get across, there's another way. About a mile along, up toward Gooseberry

Rock. The rockslide opened it up when it closed this one." He looked straight ahead.

When the pack was gone, Sheng stood up slowly. "What just happened?" he said to himself. But Bo-Bo had already broken into a run.

"Wait for me!" Sheng called. Choi Hung soared above them. They were off.

They were close to Gooseberry Rock, but Bo-Bo couldn't see the way across the canyon—until she saw a huge bush of mountain gooseberry growing at the edge. *There!* she thought. She dove into the bush. It prickled and scratched her.

"Careful, dog!" croaked Choi Hung.

Bo-Bo pushed through. There in front of her was a narrow but safe way down, down, down, and then back up again.

She barked joyfully.

"Look what you found, Bo-Bo!" cried Sheng. "We're almost there! Let's go!"

13
Crooked Cave

The path up the other side of the canyon was clear. Bo-Bo climbed it as fast as she could. She had gooseberry leaves in her fur and thistles in her paws, but she didn't care.

Because there was a cave near here. And now she suddenly knew what that cave had to be.

She had only been there once.

Her pack had known about it. It was in a gully just beyond the canyon. There was a small opening hidden by a rocky outcropping just above the gully. Thunder had taken them inside to see if there was any food or water. But there wasn't. Bo-Bo had never thought about it again.

It was the only cave close to the canyon. It must be Crooked Cave.

Bo-Bo ran up the last hill between her and the cave. Choi Hung soared above her. Sheng scrambled behind them, trying to keep up.

"We did it!" Bo-Bo barked excitedly to Choi Hung. "We found Crooked Cave!"

She reached the top of the hill and flopped down in the warm grass. She looked down into the gully.

Oh no. It can't be. Her joy vanished.

"Trouble, dog. Big trouble," Choi Hung trilled softly.

There were men everywhere. And horses. Bo-Bo heard the clang of pickaxes against rocks. She heard the cracking of rocks as they split. The men weren't using the small opening under the outcropping. They were clearing a pile of stones that hid a bigger entrance in the side of the hill. As they broke and cleared away the rocks, they propped up the entrance with wooden beams.

"Hurry up, you lazy louts!"

Bo-Bo heard a man's voice say. "Or you won't get paid a nickel."

Bo-Bo's blood turned to ice.

Mr. Smeets.

He was holding out a big piece of paper in front of him. It had marks on it. It looked like Sheng's map, only it wasn't tattered. The ringtail had said Mr. Smeets got the map last night. Bo-Bo remembered the piece of paper that had fallen out of his jacket in town. He must have made an extra copy for himself.

He'd said he had to do some things outside of town! He had horses and he'd gotten there before them.

Bo-Bo heard footsteps pounding up behind her. Sheng ran up the hill. She didn't want him to see the men at the cave. The smile on his face broke her heart. He thought they were about to find Crooked Cave. The legendary cave of gold. He thought he'd be able to pay for the bear and save the claim.

He reached the top. He stopped and put his hands on his knees to catch his breath.

"Good girl," he said. He ruffled Bo-Bo's ears. Then he peered over the edge.

The look on his face when he saw the men was something Bo-Bo didn't think she could stand. It was as though a lamp, the golden lamp that had lit up his eyes on the climb up, had gone out.

"So Mr. Smeets stole this, too," Sheng muttered. "It's not right. Nothing about this is right."

I should never have freed Resilience! Bo-Bo thought in misery. *We'd be home now, fixing supper and listening to Uncle Gwan's stories!*

But would she take it back if she could?

It's not weak to care what happens to other creatures, and to help them! she'd told Thunder. The words were still true.

It wasn't right to keep Resilience in a cage, or the ringtail on a chain!

No. Bo-Bo wouldn't undo what she'd done. Even if she could.

And she wouldn't let Smeets and his men win now.

She got to her paws.

"What are you doing?" Choi Hung squawked.

"Be quiet," Bo-Bo ordered. "I know another way in. I'm getting some gold. You keep an eye on Sheng. Make sure he stays put."

She padded along the hillside and down a narrow trail. The shelf of rock hung over the gap in the earth. It partially hid the small opening her pack had used to get inside.

She scooted through. And then she was on

a narrow ledge inside. The cave roof yawned high above her. Some of the men were inside too. They were far below her. She crawled along the ledge on her belly and looked over the side.

The men had put up more tall beams of wood to hold up the cave entrance on the inside. They'd set out lanterns to light the gloom.

There it was—gold! There were stacks and stacks of rocks, and each and every one of them glittered with veins of gold. The rocks were already mined, just waiting there on the cave floor. Men were putting them into canvas bags and taking them to the big cave entrance. All Bo-Bo had to do was get enough of them and bring them back to Sheng.

She heard heavy breathing and footsteps behind her. Her nose twitched. *Sheng!* He had followed her into the cave.

"Good girl, Bo-Bo!" he whispered. Choi Hung hovered above his head.

"I told you to keep him there!" Bo-Bo said to Choi Hung.

"Bossy, belligerent beast!" Choi Hung retorted. "*You* try to get humans to stay where they belong."

Sheng crouched down and looked over the ledge.

"Look at all that gold! We need ten ounces. Each of those rocks must have at least three or four ounces running through it! If we can even get three of them, everything will be all right."

Just then, one of the men looked up.

"Hey!" he said. "There's that kid from town!"

"He'll tell people where the cave is!" another said.

Mr. Smeets looked up.

"Get him," Mr. Smeets said. "Don't let him leave this cave alive."

14
The Battle of the Cave

Sheng and Bo-Bo turned and ran. Two men blocked their way. They must have found the hidden entrance!

"Look!" Sheng called. "That way!" Bo-Bo looked where he pointed. A zigzag path led to the cave floor and the opening held up by the beams. Maybe they could be quick enough to get past the men there.

But the men below raised their rifles. They fired.

Bullets whizzed by them and glanced off the walls and ceiling of the cave. Sheng dropped to his belly.

He pulled at Bo-Bo so she was almost flat on the ground herself. Together they crawled along the dark path to stay out of the line of fire.

More bullets. The dirt beneath them gave way. Sheng tumbled forward. Bo-Bo tried to grab his shirt, his arm, his braid, anything so she could stop him from falling. But she couldn't. He fell head over heels down the path. Bo-Bo slid after him. They landed on the cave floor.

She looked up. The men were moving toward them. They pointed their guns at Bo-Bo and Sheng.

Choi Hung dove down at the men, screeching. One of the men fired up at him. He soared out of the way and grabbed another man by his hair. The first man swung his shotgun at Choi Hung. The bird screeched again and flew high.

Sheng and Bo-Bo backed up against a boulder. They were trapped.

Bo-Bo couldn't let Sheng get hurt. She

stood, ready to charge at the men. They might shoot her, but it would give Sheng a chance to get away.

The shooting paused. The men were reloading.

And then came the only sound that could make things worse. A loud, heavy growl. Not an ordinary growl. A growl that meant it. And then a roar.

A huge grizzly bear lumbered into the cave. Its hunched shoulders were tense with fury. The ruff around its neck puffed out. When it stood up on its hind legs, it was taller than Mr. Smeets.

Choi Hung dove for the bear's head.

"No!" Bo-Bo barked. "Leave her alone!"

She knew this bear.

Resilience swept the guns out of the men's hands with one big paw. The men backed away until they hit the cave wall.

"Hello, dog," Resilience said.

"Umm . . . hello," Bo-Bo answered.

Sheng watched stock-still and wide-eyed. Choi Hung fluttered right above the bear's head.

A littler growl sounded from behind the grizzly. A small, fluffy bear face peeked out.

A moment later something furry barreled into Bo-Bo.

"You're the dog who opens cages, aren't

you?" the little bear said to Bo-Bo. "Thank you so much!"

"Errr . . . you're welcome," Bo-Bo said.

The little bear nuzzled Sheng. Very carefully, Sheng patted its head.

"You stay here, Hornet," the mama bear said to the cub. "Can you make sure he does, dog?"

"Uh . . . I'll try," woofed Bo-Bo.

"Much obliged," Resilience said.

Then she dropped down onto all fours and loped toward the rest of the men.

"Aiee!" cried one of the men. Bo-Bo recognized the one who had been selling tickets to the bear fight in town. He dropped his rifle and ran.

The others opened fire. Bullets tore into one of the beams holding up the cave entrance. It shivered.

Resilience easily dodged the shots. Bo-Bo couldn't believe how fast such a big animal could move.

Resilience stood on her hind legs again and roared. The men facing her froze in terror.

But not Mr. Smeets. He was behind the bear. She didn't see him. He cocked his rifle.

"Look out!" barked Bo-Bo. She'd promised

to watch Hornet, but she couldn't let his mother be killed. She ran at Mr. Smeets's legs as fast and hard as she could. She slammed into him. He fell.

He roared in anger just like Resilience. But he still had his gun. From the ground, he raised the rifle and pointed it at Bo-Bo. Sheng shouted, "You leave my dog alone!"

Choi Hung shrieked. Bo-Bo could only watch the gun.

Something above her chittered. A thin, sinewy shape with a long striped tail leaped down from the high ledge. It landed on Mr. Smeets's head. Its claws dug into his neck.

"YOWOWOWOWCH!" Mr. Smeets

howled. He jumped to his feet. But the ring-tail clung to his head. She swiped at his eyes. Mr. Smeets dropped his rifle and tried to pull the creature off.

"What are you doing here?" Bo-Bo barked.

"I told you I always pay my debts," the ringtail called to her. "I kept an eye on you, dog."

Mr. Smeets ran from the cave, the ringtail still on his head. His men followed.

Resilience and her cub were

snuffling around the ground. Sheng moved toward the gold-streaked rocks.

Bo-Bo heard a groaning sound. She looked up. One of the beams that held up the cave entrance creaked and swayed. It was the one the bullets had hit. It was breaking. Dust and dirt and rock rained down on them.

"The cave is collapsing!" Sheng screamed.

15
Last Chance

Resilience grabbed Hornet by the scruff and lumbered out of the cave.

"We have to get the gold!" Bo-Bo woofed to Choi Hung. She darted toward the rock pile. Sheng grabbed her by her neck fur.

"Come on, Bo-Bo!" he cried. "I don't care

about the gold anymore! I don't care about paying the tax anymore! Mr. Smeets can jump in the river with his gold in his pockets!"

He dragged her to the main cave entrance. She hadn't realized quite how strong he was. He pulled her out of the cave and into the light. Choi Hung was the last one out.

The ringtail seemed to have finally let Mr. Smeets go. Bo-Bo didn't see her. The men were swinging into their saddles. "We're leaving, Smeets!" one of them said. "We're not getting paid enough to get eaten by a bear!" They rode off. They didn't even take all the shovels.

"You get back here!" Mr. Smeets shouted. He mounted his own horse and chased after them.

The entrance to the cave shook. A wooden beam snapped. There was a great crash. Rocks and dirt and wood piled up to block the place where the opening had been.

"That was close!" Sheng said.

Bo-Bo pulled away from Sheng. They still needed the gold!

She saw that the entrance hadn't collapsed completely. There was a small hole near the top of the rocks and dirt. She ran to the cave. She wriggled through the opening.

"Stop!" Sheng desperately called out to her.

"Flea-addled, fur-brained fool!!" Choi Hung screeched.

She was inside the cave. It was so quiet, Bo-Bo could hear her own heart beating. Dust swirled in the beam of light that shone in. She ran to the stack of gold rocks.

Sheng had said they needed three.

She picked out the biggest stone. It was too big to carry. So she rolled it with her nose. It was awkward, but she kept rolling it. She got to what was left of the cave entrance. She stuck her head out of the cave and pushed the stone outside. Sheng tried to grab her. She ducked back into the cave and ran down for a second stone. She rolled that out of the cave too.

"Bo-Bo!" Sheng shouted. "Come out now!"

His hands reached through the hole to try to get her.

Just one more! She sprinted back to the rock pile.

Crack! Rumble! CRACK! The earth beneath her paws trembled. The rest of the cave was going to go any minute! She grabbed a smaller rock in her mouth. She almost dropped it. Even though it was small, it was heavier than the others.

She ran as fast as she could to the cave entrance. She dropped the rock and pushed it through the gap. Some tiny claws and some big ones, the ringtail's and Resilience's, grabbed for the rock. And it was out. She could only hope it would be enough.

The ground beneath her gave way. Another wooden beam snapped. And then another. Dirt and rocks and wood rained down on her. She winced, waiting for the cave to crush her. But just before it did, the shaking stopped. She hadn't been buried. All was quiet and darkness.

It was time to get out of there. She pulled herself up to the cave entrance.

But it was gone. Now there was a thick wall of rock between her and escape.

She was trapped.

Sheng has the gold! she thought. Even if she was trapped here forever, he would be able to pay for the tax and the bear.

But she was so afraid. *Please don't let me be trapped here forever.* She started digging. The rest of the cave could still collapse.

She heard a scratching sound. Then rocks moving. More scratching. And Choi Hung ordering everyone around. Finally, she heard the ringing of a shovel. Bo-Bo kept digging. Her paws were full of dirt and so was her nose. The cave shook again. She froze with terror.

A ray of sunlight shone into the cave. A tiny crack had appeared between the rocks. Bo-Bo couldn't believe what she saw. Acorn's

paws were digging away at the rocks. In a moment, she saw his nose. The crack grew wider as some rocks were pulled away.

Sheng's hands reached through. "I'm here,

Bo-Bo," he panted. His hands felt around for her. Bo-Bo reached with her paws. Sheng grabbed them. He pulled.

She was out. Behind her, the entrance to the cave shuddered and crashed into rocks and dust.

It didn't matter. Bo-Bo had found the gold. She hoped there was enough.

Acorn stood a few paces away. "Thank you," Bo-Bo woofed. Acorn dipped his head.

"Maybe we'll see you again sometime," he answered.

He turned and trotted away toward Scrub Hill.

A tiny warm flame sparked in Bo-Bo's

heart. The feeling spread to her face, to the tips of her ears, to her toes digging into the dirt.

But Sheng looked so upset!

"Bo-Bo!" he shouted. "Don't ever do that again!"

Why was he angry? She whimpered and flattened her ears against her head. Sheng lowered his voice.

"What were you thinking? I told you not to go! I told you I don't care about the tax anymore! Do you think gold is more important to me than you are?"

Bo-Bo hadn't thought about it that way.

"Stupid brave dog! Stupid brave dog!" Choi Hung said in human speech.

Sheng buried his head in her fur. Resilience, Hornet, Choi Hung, and the ringtail watched.

After a while, Sheng straightened up. He wiped his eyes. Bo-Bo looked at him anxiously. Was everything all right?

She woofed with relief when he smiled.

"Thanks for your help," she said to Resilience and the ringtail.

"You were kind to us," Resilience said. "Only fair for us to help you out too! Who was that other dog?"

"A friend," answered Bo-Bo. Resilience snuffled. She huffed and took off. Hornet trundled behind her. He looked back and squeaked a goodbye.

The ringtail chittered, "I'm heading back to my den. Try to stay out of trouble!"

Sheng bent to gather the rocks. Bo-Bo saw that the two bigger ones were more gold than rock! But Sheng picked up the smallest one. He stared. His mouth dropped open.

"This is almost pure gold!" He held it out in his palm. Every bit of it sparkled in the setting sun. "There must be more than a pound of gold in this," he said in a hushed voice.

Bo-Bo pointed her muzzle at the sky and barked with joy. That was much more than they needed to pay Mr. Smeets. That was more than they needed for anything!

"Come on, Bo-Bo," Sheng said. "Let's go home."

Epilogue

Bo-Bo watched Sheng put the last pack onto the wagon. The wagon was hitched to a pair of oxen Sheng's family had bought with some of the gold from Crooked Cave.

Mr. Smeets's men had told all of their friends about the cave full of gold, and dozens of men were trying to dig out Crooked Cave. But Sheng and his family didn't care.

They were leaving Gum San.

"Why stay here if the people will treat us this way?" Sheng had said when he and Bo-Bo came home with the gold. "Making you pay, Father, when other men don't have to! Just because we come from somewhere else. Just because they say we're different. And I almost lost Bo-Bo!"

Father and Uncle Gwan talked a long time. They decided Sheng was right. They gave Mr. Smeets the money for Resilience. Then they agreed together not to pay the Foreign Miner's Tax anymore. They had so much gold left over, they were going to open a store in a place called San Francisco.

Father, Sheng, and Uncle Gwan got into the wagon. Choi Hung perched on Uncle Gwan's shoulder.

Father took the reins in his hands.

"Come on, girl," Sheng said.

Father looked down at her. "Hop on up!" he said. "Can't leave without you!"

Bo-Bo bounded onto the wagon with her family. Tail wagging, she nudged everyone with her nose.

As they rattled away from their claim, Bo-Bo smelled bear.

Hidden among the trees that lined the

stream were Resilience and Hornet. Bo-Bo woofed a cheerful goodbye. They snuffled one back to her. The oxen snorted at the bears. The wagon rattled past.

"I don't think it will be easy," Sheng said to Bo-Bo. "But we'll help each other. We'll be strong enough together."

"Together! Together!" Choi Hung agreed.

Before them stretched the rolling hills, and the road to their new life.

Authors' Note

When gold was discovered at Sutter's Mill, people came from all over the world to get rich. Most did not succeed. A few people found large amounts of gold and grew wealthy almost overnight. Some found enough to make a living, especially in the first few years when the gold was easier to find. But prospecting was hard work, and even if you worked hard, you had to be lucky, too. The people who reliably made money were the ones who sold the things the miners needed. They charged extremely high prices, and the prospectors had no choice but to pay them. Many people who had spent all their money to come to California did not find much gold. They couldn't afford to go home. Some starved or died of diseases. Others kept on trying for years to find gold. Some did go home, but many others stayed, sent for their families, and settled in other parts of California.

Most of the people who came to California to search for gold were men. A few women and a few families came as well. There is no record of children coming from China, but we imagined that a strong boy, big for his age, might come to help his family.

Chinese Immigration and Racism in the California Gold Rush

Sheng's family is fictional, but we based his father and uncle on the thousands of Chinese men who came to Gum San (Gold Mountain) to try to find gold. Most were from southeastern China and were escaping war and famine. The Chinese miners would some-times work claims that white miners had given up on. At first, the Chinese prospectors were left alone by the white miners. But as more and more people came to California, and less and less gold was easily available, that changed.

The white miners began to resent people who had come from other countries. They thought the gold should belong to them. The Chinese immigrants looked different, ate different food, and spoke a language that seemed strange to the white miners. White prospectors stole their claims and threatened them. Sometimes they harassed and attacked 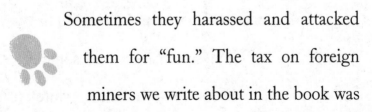 them for "fun." The tax on foreign miners we write about in the book was another way to stop the Chinese prospectors from competing for gold.

Chinese workers also came to the United States to earn money building the railroad that connected the eastern part of the nation to the western part. They were paid much less than other workers and given the most dangerous jobs. For example, at one point Chinese workers were paid 24 to 31 dollars per month while European American workers were paid 35 dollars per day.

In 1882, the Chinese Exclusion Act banned anyone from China from coming to the United States. The act was not repealed (canceled) until 1943. Even then, Congress only allowed 105 Chinese immigrants per year to enter the country. This kind of quota only ended with the Immigration and Nationality Act of 1965.

The Foreign Miner's Taxes

The tax that Sheng's family has to pay was the second foreign miner's tax. The first one, the Foreign Miner's Tax Act, began in 1850 and was $20 per month (about $400–$500 today). That tax was meant to discourage anyone from a different country from prospecting. It was quickly repealed. Then, in 1852, a new tax was created, the Foreign Miner's License Tax Act. This one was specifically aimed at

Chinese prospectors. It was the beginning of a long series of laws that discriminated against them. Many prospectors left, like Sheng's family does, and built lives elsewhere. But even after the tax was repealed, and even in cities away from the goldfields and the railroads, Chinese immigrants were subject to racist laws. For example, they could not testify against a white man in court, and they were not eligible to become citizens.

The California Gold Rush and Native Americans

The Gold Rush was a catastrophe for the indigenous people of California.

Native Americans had lived in what is now California for thousands of years before the gold-seekers came. Some of the tribes who were there for generations were the Maidu, Nisenan, Konkow, Miwok, Pomo, and Yokuts. They lived by hunting, fishing, and gathering the rich resources the land provided. When the miners came, there was competition for the land. The miners also saw the Native Americans as cheap labor.

The 1850 Act for the Government and Protection of Indians allowed Native Americans in California to be arrested and forced into slavery if they were not living on a reservation or working for a white person. Sutter's Mill is known as the place where gold was discovered, but John Sutter enslaved Native Americans even before gold was discovered.

Before the Gold Rush the Native American population was about 150,000. By 1880 it was about 30,000.

African Americans in the Gold Rush

Some African American prospectors came to California. Early in the Gold Rush, some were slaves brought to work by gold-seekers from the southern slave states. One reason that California became a free state (one that didn't allow slavery) was because the white miners who were there first didn't want southern miners using slaves and getting more gold. But that didn't mean the African American prospectors were protected. They were subjected to harassment and racist treatment. They were denied the right to vote and to testify in court. California had its own version of the Fugitive Slave Act. It allowed white slave owners to capture escaped slaves who had made it to California. Many fought against the discrimination. A man named William Sugg bought his freedom in 1854. He was part of a group of black Californians who fought for civil rights years before the Civil War started. You can visit his house in Sonora, California.

Bo-Bo's Pack

There would have been many dogs in California during the Gold Rush. Some were brought with the people who came to look for gold. There are several stories of dogs traveling on the ships that came around Cape Horn from the East Coast (a trip that could take five to eight months!). Others came over land on wagons. Many of these dogs stayed with their families, but some were abandoned when times got hard. We decided Thunder's pack would be made up of dogs left behind by prospectors.

Other Books to Read about the Chinese in California

Coolies by Yin. Illustrated by Chris Soentpiet. Puffin Books, 2003.

Oranges on Golden Mountain by Elizabeth Partridge. Illustrated by Aki Sogabe. Dutton, 2001.

Staking a Claim: The Journal of Wong Ming-Chung, A Chinese Miner, California, 1852 by Laurence Yep. Scholastic, 2013.

Acknowledgments

When we got the idea for At the Heels of History, we could only have dreamed of working with a team as skilled and supportive as the one at Margaret K. McElderry Books. Heartfelt thanks to the wonderful Ruta Rimas and Nicole Fiorica, whose editorial guidance and advice strengthened and enriched this book, and to illustrator Claire Powell, for her beautiful renderings of Bo-Bo and her world. A million thanks to the always brilliant Mollie Glick and the team at CAA.

Thank you to Eugenie Chan, acclaimed playwright of *Madame Ho*, for her cultural review of *Bo-Bo's Cave of Gold*, her insights and guidance on the lives of Chinese immigrants during the California Gold Rush, and for giving us Bo-Bo's name, and to Bonnie Akimoto for finding Eugenie for us. Thank you to author and Dance in the Spirit founder Dr. Carla Walter for advice and assistance on the experience of people of African descent during the Gold Rush. Thank you to historian Noel Cilker for being a go-to resource on the California Gold Rush and for pointing us in all the right directions for our reading. Thank you to Ed Allen at the Gold Discovery Museum and the staff at the Marshall Gold Discovery State Historic Park. Thank you to the Berkeley Public Library and Contra Costa County Library for the access to every book we could possibly need.

We could not have written this book without the guidance and support of our writing partners: Lucy Jane Bledsoe, Michelle Hackel, Mary Mackey, Lisa Riddiough, and Elizabeth Stark. Thank you to Debbie Notkin for helping us successfully navigate the world of coauthoring a creative project.

Pam would like to thank Max and Caspian for their patience and understanding while Mom was busy writing, and her husband, Mehran, and sister, Brenna, for their support and love. Dorothy would like to thank her family and friends for their love, encouragement, and support. None of this happens without all of you. Thank you to the San Francisco Writers' Grotto and Word of Mouth Bay Area. And, of course, thank you to dogs. You're all very good dogs.